Charlie's
Ice Cream Machine

First published in 2009
by Wayland

This paperback edition published in 2010 by Wayland

Text copyright © Jill Atkins
Illustration copyright © Eleftheria-Garyfallia Leftheri

Wayland
338 Euston Road
London NW1 3BH

Wayland Australia
Level 17/207 Kent Street
Sydney, NSW 2000

Series Editor: Louise John
Editor: Katie Powell
Cover design: Paul Cherrill
Design: D.R.ink
Consultants: Shirley Bickler

A CIP catalogue record for this book is available from the British Library.

ISBN 9780750258012 (hbk)
ISBN 9780750259583 (pbk)

Printed in China

Wayland is a division of Hachette Children's Books,
an Hachette UK Company

www.hachette.co.uk

Charlie's
Ice Cream Machine

Written by Jill Atkins
Illustrated by
Eleftheria-Garyfallia Leftheri

WAYLAND

It was a sunny day and everyone was hot.

Charlie and Bella were helping Dad paint the garden fence.

"I'm so hot," said Bella.
"This is a long job."
"I need an ice cream," said Charlie.

"Can you make Charlie an ice cream machine, Uncle Albert?" asked Mum.

"Oh, yes!" cried Uncle Albert.
"That sounds like fun."

He shut the door of the garden
shed and started to work.

Charlie and Bella peeped through the window.

"What sort of ice cream do you think it will make?" asked Bella.

"I bet it will be yummy!" said Charlie.

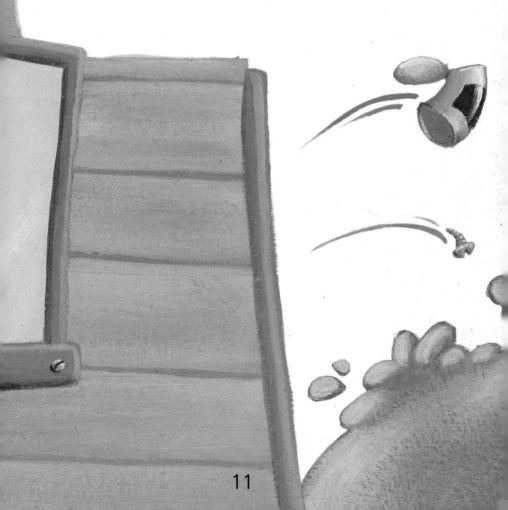

At last, the machine was ready. "I'll have a lemon one, please!" said Charlie.

Glug, glug!
Out came a scoop of
bright yellow ice cream.

Charlie licked it.

"Yuck!" he said. "It tastes
of bad egg!"

Glug, glug!
Out came a red scoop.

Bella licked it.

"This is horrible!" she said. "It tastes like ketchup!"

Glug, glug!
Suddenly, a scoop of sticky
ice cream hit Dad.

"Oops!" giggled Bella.

Glug, glug!

Splat! Another scoop landed on Mum's head.

"Oh, dear!" laughed Charlie.

"This machine is out of control!"
shouted Mum.
"Stop!" shouted Dad.

But the machine kept going.
There was ice cream everywhere.

"Do something, Albert!"
shouted Dad.

"Clean up this mess at once!"
shouted Mum.

Albert quickly turned the switch.
The machine stopped.

"I've got an idea!" he said.

Uncle Albert tipped out the ice cream mixture. Then he poured in some paint.

"It'll be much quicker to paint the fence this way!" he said to Dad.

"What a great idea!" cried Bella and Charlie. "It will be done in no time."

"And I'll just pop to the shops and get us all some ice creams," laughed Mum.

31

START READING is a series of highly enjoyable books for beginner readers. **The books have been carefully graded to match the Book Bands widely used in schools.** This enables readers to be sure they choose books that match their own reading ability.

Look out for the Band colour on the book in our Start Reading logo.

The Bands are:

Pink Band 1

Red Band 2

Yellow Band 3

Blue Band 4

Green Band 5

Orange Band 6

Turquoise Band 7

Purple Band 8

Gold Band 9

START READING books can be read independently or shared with an adult. They promote the enjoyment of reading through satisfying stories supported by fun illustrations.

Jill Atkins used to be a teacher, but she now spends her time writing for children. She is married with two grown-up children, three grandsons and a granddaughter. She loves cats and wishes she had had an uncle like Albert when she was a little girl!

Eleftheria-Garyfallia Leftheri was given a flying train for her seventh birthday. She travelled into magical worlds, where she met many mystical creatures. When she grew up, she decided to study languages so that she could talk to them, illustration so she could draw them and animation so she could make them move.